Bad Luck Bridesmaid

Maisie Moe

Bad Luck Bridesmaid

LITTLE, BROWN BOOKS FOR YOUNG READERS
www.lbkids.co.uk

With special thanks to Dan Metcalf

LITTLE, BROWN BOOKS FOR YOUNG READERS

First published in Great Britain in 2014 by Little, Brown Books for Young Readers

Copyright © 2014 by Hothouse Fiction Ltd
Series created by Hothouse Fiction Ltd
Illustrations copyright © 2014 by Clare Elsom

The moral right of the author has been asserted.

A CIP catalogue record for this book
is available from the British Library.

ISBN 978-0-349-00154-8

Typeset in Humanist by M Rules
Printed and bound in Great Britain by
Clays Ltd, St Ives plc

Papers used by LBYR are from well-managed forests
and other responsible sources.

MIX
Paper from
responsible sources
FSC® C104740
www.fsc.org

Little, Brown Books for Young Readers
An imprint of
Little, Brown Book Group
100 Victoria Embankment
London EC4Y 0DY

An Hachette UK Company
www.hachette.co.uk

www.lbkids.co.uk

My crazy family →

Dad →

Josh, my music mad oldest brother →

Mum with Arthur Stanley, my youngest and most dribbly brother (only just).

Me! Maisie Mae. ♡

The twins, Harry and Ollie. Don't even ASK.

Jack → Football mad and ALWAYS muddy. Gross.

For Posy

x

CHAPTER ONE

Food Fights and BIG ANNOUNCEMENTS

"OW! MUM!" Maisie Mae cried. It was teatime, and Maisie was sat at the kitchen table with her **BEASTLY** twin brothers Harry and Oliver. Her baby brother, Arthur Stanley, sat next to her, laughing as he smeared his face with mashed potato. Her mum was pacing up and down while she chatted on the phone.

PING!

Harry and Oliver flicked another pea at Maisie.

"Mum!" Maisie yelled again.

Mum waved her hand at Maisie to be quiet.

"Did she? She *didn't*! Well, it doesn't surprise me . . ." Mum nattered, wandering the length of the kitchen and back again.

She must have walked for **MILES**, Maisie thought.

Mum was concentrating

on the phone call, not paying attention to anything going on around her.

"Adjust elevation! Increase power for maximum devastation!" Harry said in a sergeant major voice.

"Yessir! Right away, sir!" replied Ollie, propping up his spoon on a salt cellar and re-loading it with a pea. "Ready, aim, **FIRE!**"

The pea sailed through the air and missed Maisie Mae by a few centimetres.

"Ha! Your aim's getting worse!" she said, sticking her tongue out at them.

"Be quiet and sit still, squirt, or we'll start using the mashed potato!" said Harry, waving his own spoon at her in a threatening way.

"Mum! They're bullying me with vegetables!" cried Maisie, but Mum ignored her and kept talking on the phone.

"Tell-tale!" said Ollie, picking up a big slice of carrot. He pulled his arm back and **FLUNG** it like a Frisbee at Maisie, who ducked just in time.

"Ha ha! Missed again!" she cheered, but went immediately quiet when she saw Harry and Ollie's faces drop into an *uh-oh* expression. She turned to see Dad in the doorway behind her. He had

♥ 4 ♥

a sports kit bag under each arm, and the piece of carrot stuck to his forehead.

"**BOYS!**" he yelled. "How many times? Dinner is for eating, not target practice!"

"Sorry, Dad!" the twins chorused. Josh and Jack, Maisie's eldest brothers, came in behind Dad and unloaded their bags of PE kit and musical instruments.

"My guitar lesson was **AMAZING!**" said Josh, taking off his jacket and chucking it over his guitar case. "My teacher thinks I'm nearly ready to play a full song!"

"I did **HUNDREDS** of laps of the field at football training!" said Jack, who was covered in streaks of mud. "I think I was only meant to do twenty, but I lost count."

"Right, sit up at the table. I'll get dinner sorted." said Dad as he tried to catch Mum's attention. "What are they having, Jo?"

"She won't answer you," said Maisie Mae. "She's been talking on the phone for **HOURS!**"

"Who to?" Dad asked. Just then, Mum let out an extra-loud shrieking laugh that made all the boys cover their ears. Dad looked at Maisie Mae.

"Auntie Flo!" they said together.

Mum's sister, Flo, was heaps of fun, and whenever Mum spoke to her she got all girly and giggly and excited. Maisie Mae wished *she* had a sister she could do giggly, girly things with. Instead, she had to put up with her five smelly, hairy, muddy, sweaty **BROTHERS**.

Josh was the eldest, and lived in one of

the attic rooms with Jack. He thought he was super-cool, and carried his earphones and a guitar everywhere he went. Jack was sporty and was always late for dinner, as he had a different after-school club every day. He *never* stood still and when he got too excited he would jump on the nearest person, yelling "**JACK ATTACK!**".

Next were the twins. Harry and Ollie were supreme masters in the art of **YUCK!** They could make an empty room messy and get muddy in a soap factory, which Maisie knew from when she used to share a room with them. She had been sooooo happy when she had finally got a room to herself, where the mess was all her own!

Finally there was Arthur Stanley, the baby of the family. He was all right, but if he ever filled his nappy, he could stink out a room in three seconds flat!

Maisie sighed and chomped into a fish finger as she watched Mum giggle to Auntie Flo on the phone. *I might not have a sister,* she thought. *But at least I have Bethany-next-door!*

Bethany was the same age as Maisie, the same height, and in the same class at school. They liked all the same things: glitter, Sylvanian

Families, the colour **PINK**, and making fun of *boys*. Bethany-next-door was Maisie's official best-friend-who-was-almost-as-good-as-a-sister, and she was the only person she could turn to when her awful brothers were annoying her.

"OhmygoodnessIcan'tbelieveit! That's amazing!" squealed Mum down the phone as she served up two dinners for Josh and Jack, dolloping mash and tipping out the remaining fish fingers without even looking at the plates. Dad took the plates over to the table where Josh and Jack covered their food in tomato ketchup.

"What's going on?" whispered Dad to Maisie

Mae. Maisie just shrugged, and pointed to Mum, who had finally got off the phone. She looked up with a smile.

"Pay attention everyone, I've got a **BIG ANNOUNCEMENT!**"

"Maisie's been sold to a zoo?" guessed Jack.

"Jack won a hippo look-a-like contest?" said Maisie.

"Let your mother speak!" said Dad. "What is it?"

"Wait!" shouted Josh. "Drum roll!" He started to bang on the table with his

knife and fork, until Dad wrestled them off him.

"**AUNTIE FLO IS GETTING MARRIED!**" yelled Mum. She was so excited she didn't even notice Arthur Stanley spraying food out of his mouth like a mushy pea fountain.

"Flo? *Our* Flo?" said Dad in disbelief. "Finally settling down? Crikey. Who did she manage to trick into marrying her?"

"Don't be horrible!" said Mum. "Her French boyfriend, Jean-Paul, popped the question last night!" The boys started rolling their eyes and making being-sick noises, but Mum ignored them, a dreamy look on her face.

"Oh, it's so *romantic*!" said Maisie Mae. "I can't wait to see her so she can tell us all about it!"

"Me too!" said Mum, grinning. "I said we would help her out as much as we could with the wedding. Now, here comes the *really* brilliant news!"

This got everyone's attention. Dad looked up, with his *I'm-not-sure-about-this* face. The last time Maisie had seen it was when she'd been trying to get him to let her cut Bethany-next-door's hair.

"Flo will need me around lots and lots – so I told her we'd have the wedding **HERE!**"

CHAPTER TWO

The GIRLIEST
Thing of All

"**WHOOOPEEE!**" Maisie Mae
cheered. She stood up and pirouetted
around the table in excitement, until she
got dizzy and crashed into Mum in a giggly
hug. "That's amazing!"

"Whaaaaat?" said Jack. "Does that
mean we have to tidy up?"

"Yes, it **ABSOLUTELY** does," said
Mum, smiling from ear to ear. "We're all

going to be really helpful and make this wedding the best day of Auntie Flo's life."

"I'm still waiting for the brilliant news," said Dad, whose face was frozen in fear. He seemed to be shaking too, his tea wobbling in the cup as he brought it up to his lips.

"Okay, the REAL brilliant news is that Flo and Jean-Paul can't *wait* to get married. They want a wedding as soon as possible, so I said we could do it in three weeks' time!"

Dad spat his tea out in a **SPPLLURRRTTT**.

"COOL!" The twins laughed.

"Good aim, Dad!" said Josh. "I think you got Arthur Stanley!"

Arthur Stanley looked up from his highchair, dripping with warm tea.

"Three weeks?" said Dad, rushing over to wipe down the baby. "That's *ridiculous!*"

"Yeah!" agreed Maisie. "That's ages away!" She crossed her arms and stuck her bottom lip out to make her *seriously disappointed* face.

SERIOUSLY ← DISAPPOINTED FACE

"Actually, sweetheart, that's not long at all," said Mum, helping Dad to dry Arthur Stanley off with a tea towel. "There are so many things to do! A wedding would normally take a year to organise, so we've really got to get our skates on." Mum grabbed a pad from the top of the fridge and started making lists, pacing up and down. "Let's see. There are flowers, we'll need lots of flowers! And cake, everyone likes cake."

"Ooh, yes!" said Maisie Mae, following after her, skipping with excitement. "And ribbons! And presents! And dresses!"

"We'll have to think up a colour scheme, Maisie!" said Mum. They stopped pacing and smiled at each other. "Are you thinking what I'm thinking?"

"**PINK!**" they both shouted, and collapsed into a heap of giggles. Over at the kitchen table, the boys looked horrified, while Dad put his head in his hands.

"Harry," said Ollie. "There's only one way out of this wedding. We're going to have to join the circus."

"I think you're right," said Harry. They each grabbed a handful of fruit from the fruit bowl and started to juggle them in the air.

"Flowers? Bows? **PINK?**" said Jack, dodging the flying fruit. "I'm feeling sick just thinking about it!"

"Oh, be quiet, you lot!" said Maisie. "You're just jealous because I get to

do something *girly* for once."

Maisie stopped in the middle of the kitchen as she realised

something. "Oh my goodness! Auntie Flo is almost-certainly-probably-**DEFINITELY** going to ask me to be a bridesmaid!" she said, jumping with energetic excitement, like the time she ate too many strawberry sherbets and had to run around in the garden until it wore off. She could just imagine it. *A bright sunny day. Petals and confetti floating through the air. Doves flying though the garden while she skipped through the grass in her BIG pink dress with bows and frills and ribbons.*

"**SQUEEEE!**" said Maisie, jumping up and down on the spot. "I'm **SOOOOOOOO** excited! I can't wait for MY big day!"

*

On Monday morning, Maisie Mae couldn't wait to get to school to tell everyone her super-exciting news. She was desperate to tell Bethany-next-door, who she knew would be excited for her as well. Normally she could have rushed next door to tell her straight away, but Bethany had been away all weekend visiting her ever-so-posh grandma and grandpa.

"You'll just have to wait to tell Bethany," Mum had said last night when Maisie pleaded to be allowed to phone her. "You're not joined at the hip, you know."

Maisie had gone to sleep imagining being joined at the hip to Bethany, and how **FUN** that would be! They could spend **ALL** their time together, but they would have to have funny-shaped dresses and going to the loo would be a *nightmare*.

Maisie knew that whenever Bethany-next-door came back from her posh grandparents, she always had brand-new **EVERYTHING**. It would be amazing to have something cool to tell her for once, and not just have to talk about which of her toys her brothers had managed to break over the weekend.

Mum pulled the car up outside the school.

"Have a good day, you lot!" she shouted. Harry and Ollie tumbled out, a mass of book bags, PE kitbags and lunch-boxes falling out after them. "Love you!"

"Ugh, Mum!" said Harry. "Do you *have* to?"

Maisie Mae kissed Mum

goodbye and raced out of the car, her tattered old school bag bouncing on her back. It was an old one of Jack's and had the Manchester United badge on it. It was red when it was new, but it had been washed so many times that the material was almost pink (if you squinted a bit). She dashed across the playground and over to the *cool* corner, where she and Bethany-next-door always met before school. Bethany was already there with their friends Clara and Steph.

"Morning!" puffed Maisie. "You'll never guess wha—"

"Morning, Maisie Mae!" sang Clara. "Have you seen Bethany's new rucksack? It's so **MEGA!**"

Bethany-next-door turned round so Maisie could see her brand-new rucksack.

It was really shiny, with glittery bits and sparkly tassels on the zips. And it was pink. Bright, glossy, don't-look-directly-at-it-or-you-might-get-a-headache **PINK**.

"Wow," said Maisie, forgetting about her announcement for a minute. "That's so cool!"

"**SUPER**-cool!" corrected Steph. "Where did you get it, Bethany?"

"I went to my grandma and grandpa's at the weekend. I saw it in a little shop and just *had* to have it!" said Bethany, giving a little twirl. "Grandma said

I could have it as a special Ever-So-Good Granddaughter gift."

"Amazing!" said Maisie. "Do you know what happened to me at the weekend? I—"

"What's inside?" interrupted Clara, looking at the bag. Bethany-next-door grinned like she had been hoping someone would ask. She unzipped the bag and pulled out a matching pink-princess dressing-up dress.

"It's my other Ever-So-Good Granddaughter gift!" she said, holding it up against her.

Maisie Mae gasped. It had a **HUGE** pink skirt and a picture of a princess in an oval on the front. The sleeves were puffy and ruffly, and there was a big bow at the back. It was the most beautiful

dress Maisie had ever seen. "You'll be just like a **REAL** princess!" she told Bethany. "Mum said I couldn't wear it to school," Bethany grinned, "but I could bring it in to show everyone.

What do you think?" Clara and Steph stroked the bows and ruffles.

"Oh, it's lovely, Bethany!" said Steph. "Is that real silk?"

As the others admired Bethany-next-door's dress, Maisie remembered her news. She started politely waiting until they'd finished talking so she could tell them.

"I *think* so . . ." said Bethany-next-door, looking at Maisie curiously. "Maisie, do you need the loo or something? You look like you're bursting!"

Maisie Mae jumped on the spot.

"I am, I'm **BURSTING** with news! It's been the most fantastic weekend!" she said. Finally, she had everyone's attention. "**NEWSFLASH!** I'm almost-definitely going to be a **BRIDESMAID!**"

CHAPTER THREE

A Sparkling Ring and a Tidying Fling

"Oooh! This one! This one!" said Maisie Mae, sticking a yellow post-it note with 'MM' written on it into a glossy wedding magazine.

"Maisie, you can't have *all* the dresses," said Mum. She was tearing around the kitchen with a dribbly Arthur Stanley on her hip, and piling up the kitchen table with all sorts of wedding stuff –

magazines, ribbons, napkins, menus, bits of silk and bits of lace. Maisie was beginning to think that three weeks really *wasn't* enough time to plan a wedding. Auntie Flo was arriving any minute, and they had to make loads of decisions. Luckily, Maisie was quite clear on what she wanted.

"I don't want *all* the dresses," she said. "Just the pink ones!"

Mum plonked Arthur Stanley down in a highchair and pulled a chewed bit of purple ribbon from his mouth.

"And don't forget, you haven't *actually* been asked to be a bridesmaid yet," she said.

"What?" Maisie felt a wobbly feeling in her tummy. "But I will, won't I?" she said desperately. "I mean, I'm Auntie Flo's only niece. I'm family!" Maisie imagined herself just sitting at the wedding, **NOT** being a bridesmaid, **NOT** doing anything – no flowers, no fancy shoes . . . and **NO DRESS!** Her breathing started to go a bit funny and her voice went all squeaky as she began to feel panicky. "But . . . but. . ."

"Calm down!" Mum cried. "I think it's *very* likely that Flo will ask you to be bridesmaid. But just act surprised when she does."

"Oh, I can do that!" said Maisie. She pulled her 'surprised' face, which involved opening her eyes as wide as they could go, and forming a perfect 'O' with her mouth.

EXPERT 'SURPRISED' FACE

"Hmm, you *do* look surprised," said Mum with a frown. "But more in the 'I've-just-seen-a-ghost' kind of way. Just smile and be happy. Remember, it's your Auntie Flo's big day, and *nothing* is going to ruin it."

Maisie Mae practised smiling while Mum cut out pictures from the magazines. "Oh," Mum added. "And Auntie Flo will need to sleep somewhere. Is it okay if she sleeps in your room with you?"

"*My* room? My super-cool, ultra-new, **PERFECTLY-PINK** room?" Maisie screwed up her face as she thought about it. It was only recently that her horrible twin brothers had moved up into one of the attic rooms and she'd got the room all to herself, and she didn't really want to share it. Sharing with Auntie Flo wouldn't be as bad as a load of stinky **BOYS**, though. "What about Uncle Jean-Paul?" she asked. "My room is strictly a **NO BOY ZONE**. It says so on the door!"

"He won't be here until the day before the wedding," Mum told her. "He has to stay in France while Auntie Flo comes over early to do lots of girly planning!" Maisie Mae thought about it for a minute. It's not as if Auntie Flo would spend all night snoring and trumping under the covers like the twins did.

"It's practically a bridesmaid's duty to share her room with the bride," Mum said casually. "Besides, there will be lots of girly gossip and planning. And Auntie Flo likes pink almost as much as you do!"

"Okay!" Maisie agreed. "After all, I'm almost-definitely going to be a bridesmaid, right?"

"Just wait and see." Suddenly, the doorbell rang. "Ooooh!" Mum shrieked. "She's here!"

Mum and Maisie Mae raced to open the door. Maisie flung it open to reveal Auntie Flo. She looked **AMAZING** in a long, flowing skirt and flowery, colourful top. She opened her arms wide and winked at Maisie over the top of her sunglasses.

Mum and Auntie Flo shrieked and giggled and giggled and screamed at each other for a whole minute, while Maisie watched, jiggling up and down with anticipation. Then Auntie Flo gathered Maisie Mae up in a giant hug. "Sweetiekins! You've

grown so **BIG!**" she said, pinching Maisie's cheeks. "Where did my little cuteymonster go?"

"I'm still cute!" said Maisie. Dad appeared behind them and gave Auntie Flo a hug hello.

"Ah! A big strong man! Just what I need!" said Auntie Flo, and nodded to the taxi waiting outside. The driver was unloading case after case after case from the boot onto the pavement. "Would you be a *darling*?"

"Hmm? Oh, right," mumbled Dad, and went outside to help the driver, who was grunting while trying to lift a large case out of the boot. "Crikey. Are you staying for a whole *year*?" Maisie heard him cry.

They went through to the kitchen, Mum and Auntie Flo talking to each other at a million miles an hour. Auntie Flo always had an armful of bangles and a handful of rings, as well as a few long beaded necklaces dangling around her neck, so when she moved she clattered like a set of maracas. Maisie Mae always thought that when she was older, she would wear LOTS of jewellery, just like Auntie Flo. She wondered if Auntie Flo would wear *more* jewellery for the wedding, and where it would all go? She'd have to dangle bangles from her ears, or put them round her ankles if she ran out of space on her arms.

"Let's see it then!" said Mum,

grabbing Auntie Flo's left hand. "**WOW!** It's huge!"

Maisie Mae pushed past the growing mountain of luggage that Dad was building in the kitchen, and ran over to see. On her third finger, hidden amongst the rest of Auntie Flo's large colourful rings, was a gold ring with a **MASSIVE** diamond in the centre!

Maisie Mae's mouth dropped open. "OMG, Auntie Flo! It's *gorgeous*! It must weigh a tonne!" she said. Auntie Flo smiled and kissed Maisie on the head.

"Not really," said Auntie Flo. "Would you like to try it on?"

Mum's face crinkled in an *I'm-not-so-sure-that's-such-a-brilliant-idea* way. "Um—" she started.

"Oh yesyesyesyesyesyesyes!" Maisie

Mae interrupted. "Er, *please*," she added.

Auntie Flo slipped the ring off and placed it daintily on Maisie's finger. It was too big, but Maisie fell in love with it immediately! She twirled around the room, staring into the stone in the centre, watching the light sparkle and gleam off it.

"Is it a real, real-life diamond?" she asked.

"I hope so!" laughed Auntie Flo.

"Please be careful, Maisie Mae!" Mum said, running to grab her before she twirled herself into the kitchen bin. "Flo, you'll be sleeping in with Maisie, if that's okay?"

"You know what that means, Maisie!" said Auntie Flo. "**GIRLY SLEEPOVER!**"

"Yay!" cheered Maisie. "You're the *best*, Auntie Flo!" They hugged and did a special **MWAH-MWAH** air kiss.

"There will be no sleepovers if that bedroom of yours isn't tidy," said Mum with a raised eyebrow. "You *did* tidy up, didn't you?"

Maisie gulped. She hadn't tidied in at least a week, not since she and Bethany-next-door had played an epic game of My Little Pony Beauty

Salon, with real shampoo from the bathroom.

"Um . . . Of course I have!" fibbed Maisie. "But I'll just go and check . . ."

She bounded up the stairs and burst into her room.

"Yup," she said to herself. "It's still a mess!"

Never mind, she thought. *That's what a fling-tidy is for.*

Fling-tidying was the best, funnest way of tidying **EVER**, and probably the only useful thing that Harry and Ollie ever taught her. To successfully fling-tidy, you had to do it *fast*. It was like making a mess, but in reverse. She grabbed everything off the floor and **THREW** it under the bed,

whizzing herself around the room like a whirlwind. She scooped up handfuls of dirty clothes and

HOW TO FLING TIDY
by Harry + Ollie
the awesome

TOP SECRET

RULES
Do it FAST

METHODS
Flinging, lobbing, launching, chucking, hiding, throwing, dumping

BEST TIDYING PLACES
under floorboards
under bed
out of window
in maisie's room
in wardrobe

CHUCKED them at the laundry bin. She opened her wardrobe and **FLUNG** her schoolwork into it. She pulled her pink duvet straight, and was just kicking the last Hello Kitty toy under the bed when she heard Dad coming up the stairs.

"Ready for guests?" he said.

"Of course!" said Maisie Mae, a little out of breath. Dad entered, lugging the camp bed behind him. Auntie

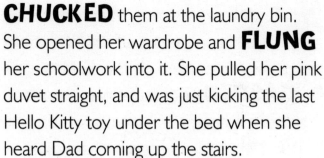

Flo followed him in. When she saw Maisie's pink walls, with the pink flowers stencilled on them, Auntie Flo **GASPED** and clapped her hands together excitedly.

"Oh Maisie Mae, this is beautiful! Just like **MY** room when I was little," she said.

"Our sleepover is going to be **THE BEST**, Auntie Flo! You can tell me all about France, and the wedding, and the honeymoon, and *everything*!" Maisie grinned.

Auntie Flo looked around the room. "I can't wait, darling," she grinned. "It's going to be so much fun. Now, let me take my ring back and let's go and get a drink."

Maisie's smile slowly faded as she looked down at her hand to see four pink fingers, one thumb, and **NO** ring.

"Uh-oh," she gulped. "It's . . . it's gone!"

MISSING

ONE SUPER SPARKLY, EXTRA SPECIALLY AMAZING BEAUTIFUL AND EXTREMELY EXPENSIVE ☆DIAMOND RING☆

GONE

ANY INFORMATION CONTACT MAISIE MAE (before I get in SO much trouble)

CHAPTER FOUR

Diamond Hunting

Maisie Mae felt the panic rise inside her. She felt shaky and a little bit sick, like the time she had accidentally glugged down one of Mum's extra-strong mocha coffees instead of her hot chocolate. She stared at the empty space on her finger, wishing and willing the ring to reappear like a magic trick.

"Gone?" repeated Auntie Flo. "What do you mean, gone?"

"I-it was here a minute ago," said Maisie, her voice wavering. "I had it before I started tidying."

Auntie Flo, who was normally tanned from her time in the French sun, had turned a shade of white that reminded Maisie of their fridge-freezer.

Dad stood completely still, and called for Mum. "Jo!" he yelled. "I think we might need you up here!"

Maisie saw the look of horror and panic on Auntie Flo's face, and knew what it meant:

1. If the ring was lost, Auntie Flo would be mega-cross.
2. If Auntie Flo was cross, there's no way Maisie would get to be bridesmaid.
3. If she didn't get to be

bridesmaid, she wouldn't get to wear any of the pretty perfectly pink dresses from the magazine.

4. This was a complete **DISASTER!**

Mum walked in, looked from Maisie to Flo and immediately knew what was wrong. "Maisie Mae, what have you done with that ring?" she sighed.

"I didn't mean to!" said Maisie helplessly. "I was just tidying, and it must have fallen off my finger!"

"G-gone?" repeated Auntie Flo.

"I think she's in shock. I'll get her a cup of tea," said Mum in a strained voice. "Don't worry, Flo, this sort of thing happens **ALL THE TIME**. It'll turn up!" She led Flo out of the door, turning to hiss at Maisie, "**FIND THAT** **RING!**"

Maisie Mae looked around at the tidy room in dismay. *Where could it be?*

"Oh dear, oh dear, oh dear!" said a voice from the door. "You've really done it now, haven't you?"

Harry and Ollie leant against the doorway with their arms crossed, smirking from ear to ear to ear to ear.

"What do you want?" snapped Maisie. "I'm busy!"

"Mum told us to come up and help you look for the diamond ring that you've lost," said Ollie. "But if you don't want our help, then we'll just go." The twins turned to leave.

Maisie sighed, but she knew what she had to do. Reluctantly, she shouted after them. "No! Wait! I need your help." The boys grinned.

"We'd love to help, but I don't think we can," said Harry, tapping on the big sign on her door which said **NO BOY ZONE**. Maisie Mae muttered under her breath and pulled the sign off. Harry and Ollie strolled in, rubbing their hands.

"So, Miss Mae," said Ollie, pretending he was a police officer. "Where did you last see the ring in question?"

"On my finger," said Maisie.

"Hmm. Maybe we should dust for fingerprints?" said Harry.

"I was wearing it before I started to tidy my room, but then it vanished," said Maisie. "You *are* going to help, aren't you? Not just point and laugh?"

Harry and Ollie exchanged glances.

"As tempting as it is to laugh at you, little sis, Mum threatened us with no Xbox for a week if we didn't help," said Harry. "So, were you tidying, or *fling-tidying*?"

"Fling-tidying," Maisie told them. "Why?"

Harry and Ollie looked at each other and shook their heads sadly.

"Rookie mistake, Maisie Moo!" said Ollie. "You should never fling-tidy while wearing expensive jewellery."

"I know that *now*!" cried Maisie. "So how do we find the ring?"

The boys' smiles grew frighteningly wide.

"There's only one thing we can do – fling-UNtidy!"

The boys whirled around the room like a twin tornado, pulling covers off the bed, turning out Maisie's toys and catapulting her schoolwork across the room. It reminded Maisie of the time her friend Steph had got a new

puppy, and she had come home to find
that it had completely destroyed the
leather sofa, with cushion stuffing and
devastation *everywhere*. Ollie chucked

clothes out of the wardrobe and onto the floor. Harry giggled excitedly as he flung the mattress off the bed.

When they had finished, Maisie Mae's room looked like a bomb had hit it. Even worse, there was no sign of the ring.

"Hmm, sorry about that," said Harry. "We did everything we could."

Maisie Mae sat down on her bed and let her head sink into her hands. "Auntie Flo is just going to *die*," she said. "And then she's going to kill me."

Harry and Ollie shared a snigger.

"You said you wouldn't laugh!" moaned Maisie.

"Calm down, Monkey Mae!" said Ollie. "We *did* find this. Any good?" He opened his hand to reveal a bright, shining diamond ring.

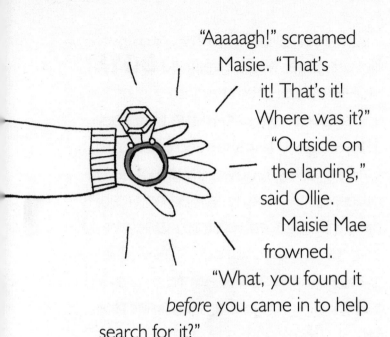

"Aaaaagh!" screamed Maisie. "That's it! That's it! Where was it?"

"Outside on the landing," said Ollie.

Maisie Mae frowned.

"What, you found it *before* you came in to help search for it?"

The boys nodded.

"*Before* you turned my room upside down?"

They nodded again.

Maisie Mae gave a terrible roar as she chased them out of the room and down the stairs.

"You complete and utter, beastly, bothersome, bogie-breathed **BOYS!**"

All three of them ran into the kitchen and skidded to a halt on the tiled floor. They crashed together and Harry and Ollie fell straight down on top of each other. As his brother landed on top of him, the ring tumbled from Ollie's hand and flew across the floor. Maisie Mae grabbed it and was at Auntie Flo's side in a second, an angelic smile on her face.

"Found it!" she chirped.

"Oh, thank goodness!" said Mum. "Did the twins help?" They all looked over to Harry and Ollie, who were laid out on the floor in a heap.

"No," said Maisie, rolling her eyes. "They didn't help *at all*. You know what boys are like."

As Ollie and Harry protested, Mum man-handled them out of the kitchen. "I told you to help your sister! No Xbox for a week!" she commanded, to a series of groans from the boys. Auntie Flo pushed the engagement ring back into place on her finger.

"Ah, that's better!" she sighed.

"Auntie Flo, I'm **SUPER** very, very, sorry about the ring. It won't happen again. I feel really guilty—" Maisie started.

"Shhhh," hushed Auntie Flo. "There's no harm done. Actually, I'm glad we're alone, Maisie Mae." Auntie Flo said, making her voice all quiet and secretive and pulling Maisie in for a hug. "There is something very important I've been meaning to ask you."

Excitement bubbled up inside Maisie
Mae like one of Arthur Stanley's burps.

"Would you do me the honour
of being my bridesmaid?" Auntie Flo
asked.

Yeeeaaahhh!

said
Maisie
Mae, almost
hitting the ceiling
as she leapt
in the air.
"Woo-hoo!
Yes, please! Oh
thankyouthankyouthankyouthankyou!"

Auntie Flo laughed as Maisie flung her arms around her. "I won't let you down," Maisie declared. "I'll be the best bridesmaid **EVER!**"

Auntie Flo managed to interrupt her. "Woah there! That's not all!" she said.

That's not all? thought Maisie Mae. *That's the most best, fantastically life-changing news I've had since forever. What else could there be?*

"I've got a little surprise that I think you'll like," said Auntie Flo with a smile. "I'm going to ask your best friend, Bethany, to be a bridesmaid too! What do you think to that?"

Maisie Mae stopped dead. *Bethany-next-door, a bridesmaid?* she thought. *But I wanted to be the bridesmaid! It won't be*

*so special if Bethany-next-door gets to be
one as well.*

"Maisie?" said Auntie Flo. "Are you
okay? What do you think?" She looked at
Maisie with a smile so wide that Maisie
thought her face might crack.

"That's . . ." said Maisie. "That's . . .
that's great!" Maisie hugged her auntie
again.

But . . . but . . . but . . . she thought to
herself, *it's* **SOOOO UNFAIR!**

CHAPTER FIVE

Bedtime Chat

Maisie Mae lay in bed that night, her pink duvet pulled up tight under her chin, her eyes open, wide awake. Auntie Flo was next to her on the tiny camp bed, tossing and turning in her sleep. Even though she had taken all her rattly jewellery off, she was making more noise than when she was awake! She grunted and groaned, and occasionally muttered something in French.

It's still better than sharing a room with Harry and Ollie, thought Maisie.

Auntie Flo wasn't the reason Maisie Mae couldn't sleep, though. She just kept thinking about the moment when Auntie Flo had told her that Bethany-next-door was going to be a bridesmaid too.

Bethany-next-door had already been a bridesmaid twice before! Once when her cousin Toby got married in Scotland and she had to wear a tartan dress with huge white stockings and learn funny Scottish dances, and another time when her Mum's best friend's sister's daughter-in-law got married. That time the bride had had *twelve* bridesmaids. Both times Bethany-next-door had got to keep the dress *and* a bouquet of flowers, and she had talked about it in the playground for

WEEKS. Maisie Mae had *never* been a bridesmaid, and even though Bethany-next-door was her bestest-ever-friend-in-the-whole-wide-universe, she wanted to do it by *herself*.

Auntie Flo let out a loud snort.

Maisie Mae sighed. She'd never get to sleep with **THAT** noise going on next to her! She pulled back the covers, slid her feet into her pink rabbit slippers, and tiptoed downstairs.

Normally she wasn't allowed out of bed past bedtime, but 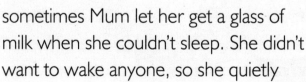 sometimes Mum let her get a glass of milk when she couldn't sleep. She didn't want to wake anyone, so she quietly pushed the kitchen door open. But the light was on anyway. Mum was in there, rocking slowly backwards and forwards with Arthur Stanley over her shoulder like a bag of spuds. She held her finger up to her lips to tell Maisie to be quiet.

"Has he gone to sleep?" mouthed Mum, turning away so Maisie Mae could see the baby's face. His eyes were screwed up tight and a long line of drool was leaking out of his mouth and down Mum's back. Maisie nodded, and Mum placed him carefully down in a bouncy baby chair. "And what can I do for you, Madam?" Mum asked.

"Couldn't sleep," shrugged Maisie. "Auntie Flo snores."

"I know," said Mum, reaching for the milk without even being asked. "I used to share a room with her when we were little. We used to have the most awful fights!"

"Worse than me and the boys?" said Maisie Mae.

"Hmm, I'm not sure about *that*," said Mum. Maisie sat down at the kitchen table and Mum slid a glass of milk across to her. "So, how are you feeling about being a bridesmaid?"

"Oh, um . . . really excited," said Maisie in the most unexcited voice ever. She let out a little sigh.

"But . . . ?" Mum asked.

Maisie sipped at her milk and then let it all out.

"It just **UNFAIR!** I don't want Bethany-next-door to be a bridesmaid. I want it to be **MY** day, and for it to be extra-specially special!"

Mum nodded and stroked Maisie Mae's hair, running her fingers through her curls.

"I understand, sweetheart, but don't you think being a bridesmaid will be even more fun when you've got your best-friend-who-is-almost-as-good-as-a-sister to share it with?" said Mum. "Auntie Flo knew that there would be lots of grown-ups about, and that you might get lonely if you didn't have a friend there to have fun with. Otherwise you'll just have your *brothers* to play with." Mum made a funny face, like she knew how **AWFUL** that would be.

Maisie Mae glugged down her milk. *Getting dressed up with Bethany-next-door would be kind of fun,* she thought. *And they could dance together and throw confetti, and have fancy drinks with bits of fruit stuck in the top and little cocktail umbrellas . . . Mum was right! She always had a super-fun time with Bethany-next-door. Having her best friend at the wedding would be great!*

"Yeah." Maisie grinned. "Thanks, Mum!"

Mum kissed the top of her head and they both went up to bed, Mum carrying

a snoring Arthur Stanley. Maisie yawned
as she climbed the stairs, feeling all excited
again. This was going to be the best
wedding in the history of the universe!

After a good night's sleep, Maisie woke up
from dreams of dresses and confetti and
almost catapulted herself out of bed onto
her Auntie Flo.

"Aaagh!" screamed Auntie Flo, startled. "Oh, good morning, Maisie Mae."

"No!" said Maisie. "It's a **GREAT** morning! Bright and sparkling with chocolate sprinkles on top!"

"Erm . . . If you say so," yawned Auntie Flo, groggily.

Maisie Mae was in a good mood. The **BEST** mood! She couldn't wait to tell Bethany-next-door that she could be a bridesmaid too!

It took *ages* for Maisie Mae to get her aunt and her mum awake enough to go next door and tell Bethany. Auntie Flo had insisted on brushing her hair and her teeth and everything before she was ready to go. *Eventually,* they went next door.

"I'll do the door!" called Maisie Mae. "Bethany and I have a special coded door-knock. It used to be a special ring, but the bell has mysteriously stopped working. I think the postman broke it."

Maisie knocked slowly four times, then ended with a long drumroll with her knuckles. The door opened and Bethany-next-door's mum stood in front of them, looking as sleepy and tired as Mum and Auntie Flo.

"Morning," mumbled Mum. "This is my sister, Flo,"

"I need to talk to Bethany!" Maisie Mae burst past Bethany's mum and ran up the stairs two at a time, then exploded into Bethany's room. It was as pink and tidy as always, with everything neatly in its place. The only thing that wasn't there was Bethany.

"Bethany?" Maisie called.

 72 ♥

"Ah'm in 'ere," came a burbly call from the bathroom. Maisie Mae barged in. Bethany-next-door was already dressed, with her perfect blonde hair in plaits. She was brushing her teeth with her Barbie toothbrush, bubbles spilling from her mouth like she'd just eaten a soap sandwich.

"You'll never guess what!" said Maisie in her extra-loud, extra-high pitched excited voice. "**AUNTIE FLO IS GETTING MARRIED IN OUR HOUSE NEXT DOOR AND SHE WANTS ME TO BE A BRIDESMAID AND SHE WANTS YOU TO BE ONE TOO!**" she blurted in one breath.

SPLURT! Bethany-next-door spat her toothpaste all over the bathroom mirror in shock.

"No *way*?" she said, dropping her toothbrush in amazement.

"*Yes* way!" said Maisie. The two of them started squealing with joy and jumping up and down. "You and I, Bethany, are going to be the best bridesmaids **EVER!**"

CHAPTER SIX

Dressing Up

"Do you think she's stuck?" said Bethany-next-door. "That happened to my mum once. She was trying on an old pair of jeans and couldn't get them off. We had to cut her out with the kitchen scissors in the end. She doesn't really like it when I tell people that story."

Maisie Mae paced up and down the lounge, wearing a groove in the carpet.

It was only a day until the wedding now, after a few short weeks living in wedding HQ. The wedding had been planned down to the finest detail, and it was all that anyone had talked about. But today something amazingly exciting was going to happen – she was going to see **THE DRESS** for the very first time. And she was going to see Auntie Flo's dress too.

"They've probably forgotten about us! I mean, how long does it take to get dressed?" Maisie Mae complained, looking at the clock for the sixty-bagillionth time. The hands didn't seem to have moved at all.

"I think that clock's broken," Bethany said grumpily. "It probably died of boredom."

Maisie went to the bottom of the stairs and yelled up. "Mum! What's taking so long?"

"You can't rush perfection!" Mum called back. "So hold your horses!"

Maisie stomped back to the lounge in a grump. It was a stupid saying, especially as she'd asked Mum and Dad *loads* of times for her very own horse and they had refused, saying that the garden wasn't big enough. Just then, they heard a creak on the stairs, and some nervous mutterings from Mum and Auntie Flo.

"Don't step on it!"

"I'm not! Just watch your feet!"

"I can't see my feet!"

Maisie held her breath in excitement. She was **DYING** to see the wedding dress, and she felt all nervous for Auntie Flo, like she had butterflies in her tummy. Actually, it was like she had butterflies, moths, crickets, grasshoppers and cockroaches all squirming around in there.

"Ready, girls?" called Mum from around the corner.

"**READY!**" they chimed.

Auntie Flo floated through the door in a long, flowing white dress. It was the most beautiful and

ENORMOUS dress Maisie had ever
seen! It was *so* Auntie Flo. It had
ruffles and frills, satin and lace,
crinkly bits and crumply
bits, sequins and sparkly bits.
The skirt was so huge and puffy
that if it rained, Maisie and Bethany-next-
door could hide underneath it to stop
getting wet. But Auntie Flo's smile was
even **BIGGER**.

"Oh, Auntie Flo!" breathed Bethany
in a dreamy way. "It's *gorgeous*!"

Mum came around the corner holding
up two smaller, pinker dresses. "And what
do you make of these, girls?" she said with
a smile.

"**SQUEEEEEEE!**" Maisie
Mae and Bethany-next-door
shrieked at the same time.

They charged Mum to get their hands on the dresses. Maisie grabbed hers and held it tight like it was a baby.

"It's perfect!" she said. "It's so pretty! And it's **PINK!**" She put her cheek up to the soft silky fabric.

"Can we try them on?" said Bethany-next-door.

"Pleasepleasepleasepleasepleeeeassseee!" added Maisie.

"Go on then!" said Mum.

"Don't be too long!" said Auntie Flo. "I can't sit down in this dress!"

A wave of excitement crashed over Maisie as she grabbed Bethany's hands and they jumped up and down.

"**TEAM BRIDESMAID!**" Maisie yelled. "**GO, GO, GO!**"

They ran up the stairs to Maisie's room
and flung their tops and skirts over the
bed, clambering into the dresses. Maisie
got her head stuck in an armhole and her
arm stuck in the head hole, and had to be
rescued by Bethany.

When she eventually got into the

dress, she and Bethany-next-door gazed at each other in wonder, then rushed into the lounge to show Mum.

"Oh, Auntie Flo! Thank you! They're the **GIRLIEST** dresses in the whole entire world!"

"Hmm. They'll need a bit of taking in," said Mum. "You'll have to stand still while I pin it up."

Maisie grabbed the nearest part of Mum she could get, which was her leg, and hugged her tight. "Mum, it's the nicest dress I've ever worn!" she said, stroking the material. "I love it so so so so **SOOOOOO** much!"

Mum freed her leg from Maisie's grip and then got her to stand on top of a chair. She took out her sewing kit and began hunting for some pins. Maisie ran her hand along the smooth material and sang a little tune from her Nana's old music box, while she twirled

around like a ballerina, making Auntie Flo and Bethany-next-door laugh.

"Stand **STILL**, Maisie Mae!" mumbled Mum through

a mouthful of pins. When Maisie was all pinned up, she was allowed to get down and practice her bouquet-catching with a bunch of rolled-up socks while Bethany took her turn to stand on the chair.

"Girls, you look like princesses!" said Auntie Flo. She had prised herself out of the wedding dress and was now walking about in a dressing gown with a cup of tea. "Bethany, you look picture perfect! Just wait until we get the posy of flowers for you to carry." Auntie Flo ran a brush through Bethany-next-door's hair and smiled. "Oh! I almost forgot!"

She rushed out of the room and came back with two small boxes.

"A princess wouldn't be a princess without her tiara!"

Auntie Flo gave Maisie Mae her box

and smiled eagerly as she opened it.
Maisie gave a yelp of delight when she
saw a perfectly perfect, **PROPER**
silver tiara, studded with gorgeous twinkly
DIAMONDS!

"Oh . . . my . . . goodness!" she
squealed, too excited for words. "It's
the most beautiful thing I've ever seen!
My own diamonds! Is it very rare and
expensive? Like a family heirloom?"

"Um, not *exactly*. They're diamanté,"
said Auntie Flo. "I got them off eBay."

"Diamanté," Maisie sighed happily.
She looked over to see Mum
unwrapping an identical tiara, and
placing it on Bethany-next-door's head.
Bethany squeaked with glee as the tiara
sat perfectly on her straighter-than-
straight blonde hair.

← ACTUAL
DIAMONDS!

Auntie Flo put the
other tiara on Maisie's
head and it immediately
sank into her mass of

← ACTUAL
~~DIAMONDS!~~
DIAMANTÉ!!

brown curly hair. She had to lift the mirror
up high to even get a glimpse of the
diamantés. Auntie Flo moved over to fuss

over Bethany. Maisie Mae tried to flatten her curls down while Bethany got all the attention. She couldn't help but feel a little jealous of her best friend. Eventually, Mum came over to help.

"Hmm, maybe if we tame that mane of yours . . ." said Mum. She reached for a special comb that Maisie called *The Tangle Eater*. Maisie winced as Mum ran the comb through her hair, pulling hard to try and get it to behave.

↑ The Tangle Eater

"Ow. Ow! OW!" said Maisie, wriggling as Mum yanked and tugged her hair. This was **NOT** how being a perfectly perfect bridesmaid-princess was supposed to feel. She was about to squirm free and make a run for it when she saw something that made her stop dead.

"Ah!" said Mum. "Finally, you've made it! Let's have a look then!"

The door opened slowly and in slouched Josh, Jack, Harry and Ollie, looking like they wanted the ground to open up and swallow them as they stood in the centre of the room wearing their brand-new, super-shiny **PINK** pageboy suits!

CHAPTER SEVEN

Marquee Mayhem

"Bwa-ha-ha-ha-ha-ha-ha-ha-ha-ha-ha-haaaaaaaaaaaaaah!" laughed Maisie Mae.

"Hee-hee-hee-he-he-he-he-hee-hee-heeeeee!" squealed Bethany-next-door.

Maisie Mae laughed and laughed and laughed and laughed. She also giggled, guffawed, chortled and chuckled. The boys all stood in a row, looking completely cheesed off.

"Finished?" said Jack finally.

"Oh no!" said Maisie Mae. "I'm going to be laughing about this for a loooong time."

"You all look so *sweet*!" said Bethany, smiling at them in their identical **PINK** suits. "Like a boy band from Barbieland!"

The twins exchanged a glance.
They looked each other up and down,
shuddered with disgust, and looked away
again.

"Maisie Mae, I can't tell you how
important this is. This goes for you
too, Bethany," said Ollie.

"If you tell anyone at school about
this, we will **KILL** you until you are
DEAD!" said Harry.

"We won't *say* a single word!"
promised Maisie Mae. She leaned over
and whispered in Bethany's ear.
"We'll just show everyone the
photos!"

"Okay, everyone!" yelled Mum.
"We're going to have a rehearsal now!
Places, please!"

Mum pushed and pulled and arranged

everyone into the right order. The boys shuffled and stomped down the hallway miserably as Mum hummed 'Here Comes the Bride'. "Dum, dum DE dum. Dum, DUM, de, dum! Pick your feet up, Josh! Dum dum de DUM DUM, de dum dum de DUM! Don't slouch, Jack!"

Maisie Mae and Bethany-next-door took their places and walked slowly and gracefully down the hallway after the boys.

"Perfect, girls!" cheered Mum. "You look wonderful!"

Maisie and Bethany looked at each other and giggled. This was **SO** much fun!

They marched through the kitchen and out of the patio doors, into the garden.

"Whoa!" said Bethany-next-door as she stepped onto the grass.

"Double whoa!" said Maisie Mae. At the end of the garden was a **HUGE** white tent, with pretty twinkly fairy lights strung all the way around it. Dad stood at the entrance with a cup of tea and a rubber mallet, looking tired and pleased. The boys all ran over.

"Cool!" said Josh. "Nice tent, Dad!"

"It's a *marquee*," corrected Dad. "A very *expensive* tent. This is where everyone will be having dinner after the wedding."

Maisie Mae and Bethany-next-door followed the boys inside, where they *oooohed* and *aaaahed* at the decorations. Dad had put fairy lights all around, and outside the door were lots of picnic candles. There were tables and chairs everywhere, and Dad set the boys to work lifting them into place, while the girls moved on to a slippy slidey wooden floor at one end of the tent.

"This is the dance floor," said Bethany, knowledgeably.

"Turn the lights on! Turn the lights on!" said Maisie, and Dad went over to a tangle of cables and flicked a switch. The fairy lights lit up, and both the girls squealed with delight. It was like fairyland! "It's **AMAZING!**" said Maisie Mae. "Can't we have a tent in the garden all the time?"

"A *marquee*," said Mum. "It wouldn't be very special if we did, would it?" Just then, Mum's mobile phone rang.

"Hello? Yes, speaking. . . What? No! I said *lilies*! No, no, **NO!**" she said, sounding panicky. She held the phone away from her mouth. "It's the florist! There's a flower emergency!" She started to walk back to the house with Dad and Auntie Flo following behind her. Just before she got inside Mum turned and shouted back to the boys.

"Don't mess up your suits!" she ordered, wearing her 'I'm-absolutely-**SERIOUS**' face. "If anyone does anything to get even a speck of mud on them, you will be in more trouble than you've *ever* been before."

"Don't worry," said Josh. "We'll stay in the tent."

"It's a **MARQUEE**!" shouted Mum and Dad, before they disappeared into the house.

About four seconds later, Josh turned to his brothers.

"Okay, they're gone," he said. Harry and Ollie dropped the table they were carrying. "I'm off!" Josh stormed out of the side gate. Jack groaned and slumped down into a dusty corner.

"This is a nightmare!" he said. "A fluffy, twinkly, flowery, fairy pink, **GIRLY** nightmare!"

"It's fun!" said Maisie Mae. She and Bethany-next-door were on the dance floor, swirling around like they'd seen people do on

Strictly Come Dancing. "At least we get to dance!"

"Hmm," said Harry. "That's true!" He and Oliver

grinned at each other, then ran over, falling down on their knees and skidding the entire length of the dance floor. "**ROCK AND ROLL!**" they screamed, nearly knocking over Maisie and Bethany.

"Ugh! Stupid boys!" said Bethany-next-door. "Always spoiling things! There is no **WAY** I'm going to get *my* dress dirty."

"Certainly not!" said Maisie Mae,

putting on her poshest voice. She turned to Bethany-next-door with a grin. "Why, if it isn't Duchess Bethany de Bumbum! My dear, I haven't seen you in simply ages!"

Bethany-next-door giggled. "Lady Maisie Mae Crinklebottom!" she replied in her best princess voice. "What a delight! Would you care for tea?"

"Oh, I don't mind if I do! Our usual table, please, Alfred!" Maisie said to an imaginary waiter. *Being a fancy lady is so much fun!* she thought as she and Bethany swanned over to a table and sat down. They even brushed off the seat so they wouldn't get dust on their dresses.

They played at being fancy ladies a bit longer, eating imaginary cucumber sandwiches and discussing the *awful* weather they've had recently, but Maisie couldn't help thinking that it wasn't much fun without real food and drink. Just then, she spied a big pile of drinks in the corner that Dad had got from the supermarket. There was all sorts there – wine and cans of beer for the grown-ups and soft drinks for the kids. She even spotted a box **FULL** of Ribena cartons.

Her mouth watered at the sight of them, and then realised that everyone had been so busy with the wedding that she hadn't had a drink since breakfast.

"Bethany," she said. "We wouldn't get into terrible trouble if we were to help ourselves to a carton, would we?"

"Um . . . I'm not sure," said Bethany-next-door, but Maisie was already out of her seat and walking over to the tower of drinks. She ripped the box open and grabbed a Ribena each for her and Bethany. She went back to the table and continued with her acting.

"Now, where were we?" she said in her posh voice. Bethany-next-door opened her Ribena and sipped at it carefully with one little finger stuck out like she was at a *proper* tea party.

"Mmm! What delicious wine!" she said, and swilled it around in her mouth. "I'm tasting grapes . . . I'm tasting strawberries, I'm even tasting . . . **BOGIES!**"

Maisie Mae **BURST** out
laughing and sprayed her mouthful of
Ribena everywhere! Bethany giggled
uncontrollably too, but stopped dead
when she looked over to Maisie.

"What? What's the matter?" said Maisie
Mae, seeing the look of **HORROR** on
her face. Maisie looked down and gasped.
Her perfect **PINK** flouncy dress was
covered in spots of purple
Ribena!

CHAPTER EIGHT

CRISIS!

Maisie Mae stared down at her beautiful pink dress, and at the spots of purple drink that were spreading quickly over her tummy.

"No!" she whispered in a panic. "No, no, no, no, **NOOOOOOOO!**" She looked up to Bethany-next-door, who was staring at the dress with her mouth wide open. "It'll be okay!" Maisie gulped. "Won't it?"

"Y-yes, of course!" Bethany said finally. "Y-you can hardly n-notice it!"

Maisie Mae dropped the carton of drink and started to cry big, uncontrollable tears.

"I . . . just . . . wanted . . . to . . . be . . . a . . . bridesmaid!" she said in between sobs. "Now . . . it's . . . all . . . ruined!"

"What's wrong, Maisie?" Jack asked, coming over to see her. "Uck-oh," he added as he looked at the dress. "I think we need to go and show Mum," he said softly.

Maisie looked up in horror. "No!" she said. "I can't! She'll never let me be a bridesmaid again, **EVER!**" She wiped her tears away with her hands. "Please don't tell her, Jack, *please*!"

Jack put his hands up. "Okay, okay! But what are you going to do? The wedding is less than twenty-four hours away, and you can't be a bridesmaid with your dress like that."

"That's **LOADS** of time!" came a voice from behind them. They turned to see Harry and Ollie, looking Maisie Mae over with an impressed look on their faces. "I've got

to hand it to you, Maisie," said Harry. "I never even thought that if we ruined our suits we'd be out of the wedding. Good plan!"

"B-but . . ." stammered Maisie Mae, "I want to be in the wedding more than **ANYTHING!**"

"Hmm . . ." said Oliver. "In that case, you're a bit stuck."

"The way I see it, you have two choices," said Harry.

"One, we give you one of our suits to wear. No one will notice a thing!" said Oliver.

Maisie Mae shook her head. "I'm a **GIRL!**" she told them.

"Okay, okay! That leaves option two. We take the dress and use our tried and tested technique of stain matching."

"What's that?" Maisie sniffled.

"We get stains on our clothes all the time," said Oliver. "But Mum never notices because of our patented stain-matching technique."

"We find stains which match the colour of our clothes and cover up the original stains! It's easy, when you've had the practice that we've had," said Harry.

Maisie swallowed down a sob. "Would you do that for me? Really?"

"Maisie Mae!" laughed Harry. "What are big brothers for?"

Maisie thought that big brothers were for putting snails under your duvet when you weren't looking, or stealing your My Little Pony toys and gluing Action Man guns on them to turn them into

Unicorns of Death, but she stayed quiet. Just then, they heard Mum coming  A Unicorn of Death

back through the kitchen. In the tent, everyone started to panic.

"**QUICK!**" said Harry. "You run inside and change. We'll meet you in your room."

"Mum will see me!" said Maisie Mae.

"Trust us," said Oliver. "She won't be looking at your dress!"

Jack gathered up the Ribena cartons and stuffed them in a nearby bush, while the twins dashed onto the grass and began to pass a football to each other. Maisie Mae and Bethany-next-door marched quickly towards the patio doors. Maisie crossed her arms in front of her to try and hide the Ribena splatter. Mum stepped through the doors and glanced at Maisie. Just when Maisie thought her time as a bridesmaid was completely and definitely over, there was a noise from behind her.

"**HARRY! OLLIE! NOOOO!**" Mum yelled.

Maisie turned just as Harry passed the football to Oliver, who skilfully managed to hit one of the pegs that held the giant tent in place. With a **TWANG!** the rope became unfastened and one side of the tent collapsed in on itself, followed by a scream from Mum.

"My **MARQUEE**!" Mum shrieked. Maisie smiled and rushed past her, completely unnoticed.

Up in Maisie's room, Bethany-next-door helped her take off the dress and carefully laid it out on the bed. Maisie got into a t-shirt and skirt and looked over the damage.

"It's bad isn't it?" she said to Bethany. "It looks like a blackberry bush exploded over me."

All Bethany could do was nod.

TWANG!

There came a knock at the door, which Maisie recognised as Harry and Oliver's special code — four knocks, three taps, two scratches and a kick. She let them in.

"Can you fix it?" she asked immediately. The boys looked over the dress.

"I think we might be able to come up with something!" said Oliver. "I'm thinking strawberry sauce might do the job, or perhaps even a juicy, ripe raspberry?"

"We'll get it back to you as quick as a flash!" said Harry. He grabbed the dress and dragged it upstairs to the twins' den.

Maisie and Bethany-next-door looked at each other as they heard the door slam above them, and footsteps bang on the ceiling like they were teaching a rhino to tap-dance. Then there was a slamming of doors and the sound of the twins racing

up and down the stairs. Bethany, being
the bestest-friend-that-ever-there-was,
tried to take Maisie Mae's mind off what
was being done to her dream dress by
fishing the tiara out of her curly hair and
giving her a new hair-do.

All the fussing and preening didn't distract
Maisie from the sounds of mayhem upstairs.

"What's taking them so long?" said
Maisie Mae. "It's been hours!"

"It's been twenty-three minutes," corrected Bethany-next-door. "Here they come now!"

There was a tumble of feet down the stairs, and then the secret knock on the door. Maisie flung the door open.

"Well?" she said, frantically looking around. Harry stood behind Oliver, and clutched something behind his back.

"Maisie, I want you to know that we did everything we could," said Oliver.

"Show me," Maisie said nervously.

"You're not going to like it," said Harry.

"Show me!" Maisie Mae screeched.

The boys entered and spread the dress out on the bed. Bethany-next-door gave a gasp of shock when she saw it, while Maisie Mae just stared and stared, her mouth wide open in amazement.

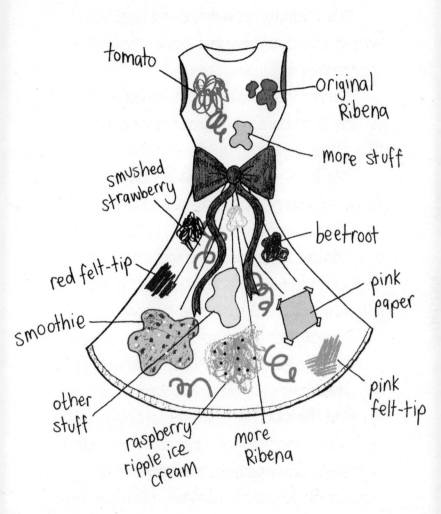

tomato

original Ribena

more stuff

smushed strawberry

beetroot

red felt-tip

pink paper

smoothie

other stuff

raspberry ripple ice cream

more Ribena

pink felt-tip

"What's that?" She pointed at a blotchy purple splat on the dress.

"Beetroot. Bit too dark."

"And that?" she stabbed at a red patch.

"Red felt-tip. Didn't work as well as I thought it would."

The dress was a **DISASTER**. There were splots and splashes everywhere. Ribena stains now mixed with beetroot, felt-tip, tomato sauce and smushed strawberry. There were ten different types of pink, but none of them matched the dress.

"It's not *that* bad," said Harry.

Maisie finally flipped. "Not that bad?" she yelled. "It's awful! I can't wear that! It's **RUINED!**" She lunged at her brothers. Harry and Ollie made a run for it, scampering upstairs. Maisie flomped down onto her bed. Bethany-next-door sat next to her. They were both silent for a second. Then Bethany-next-door came up with a **BRILLIANT** idea. "We could try washing it!"

It was such a simple plan that neither of them had thought of it until now. Maisie perked up.

"Bethany, you are a **GENIUS!**"

They both ran downstairs and grabbed Jack. Mum always made him put his stinky sports kit straight in the washing machine, so he *must* know how it worked.

"You *have* to help us!" Maisie said, pulling him up by his wrists. "We need to put this in the washing machine, but it's all dials and letters and buttons!"

Jack helped them fill the washing machine the way he did with his sports kit.

"Mum always makes me put it on a

really high temperature to get rid of the stains," he explained. "I've put my muddy football kit in there as well, so she won't get suspicious about what we're washing. Ready?" he said. He pressed the button and the washing machine whirred into life.

"This better work," whispered Maisie Mae to herself. "Or it's bye-bye bridesmaid!"

CHAPTER NINE

Disasters and Miracles

The monster was **HUGE** with a gooey, melted green face and terrifying twisted hair.

"Maisie Mae! Maisie Mae!" it groaned. A long arm reached out its claws and shook Maisie awake from her dream. She rubbed her eyes and realised it was just her Auntie Flo with a mud-pack smeared over her face, her hair in curlers and her

fingernails painted. She was shaking Maisie
and shouting excitedly.

"Wake up, wake up, Maisie Mae! It's
my wedding day!" she trilled.

Maisie was suddenly wide awake.
As Auntie Flo disappeared in a cloud of

perfume, she could only think about one thing: her bridesmaid dress. There hadn't been time to check it during the evening because the wash had taken *ages*. Jack had set the machine to dry as well, which took even longer. She needed to know if her dress was okay, or if she was going to be grounded until she was too crinkly and old to be a bridesmaid.

She threw on her dressing gown and slippers, and tiptoed down the stairs. When she reached the bottom, she looked around to see if she had accidentally come down a different set of stairs into the wrong house. The whole place looked **AMAZING**.

Everywhere she looked was decorated in pink-and-white bows and ribbons, with flowers on every surface. Mum was already up and in her special long dress, and with a big hat with lots of flowers and twiddly bits on it. She was fiddling with a bunch of white flowers, and turned to see Maisie, who had her mouth open in astonishment.

"It's . . . it's . . . **BEAUTIFUL!**" said Maisie.

"Thank you, Maisie Mae!" smiled Mum. "Not in your dress yet?"

Maisie gulped.

"I, er . . . didn't want to spill my breakfast on it!" she said.

"Good idea!" said Mum, and went back to fussing with the flowers.

Maisie went through to the kitchen and checked that she was alone. She knelt down to the washing machine and held her breath as she opened the door. All she could see was Jack's football kit, so she stuck her hand in and rummaged around until she found something pink. It was the ribbon from her dress! *Maybe it's okay?* Maisie thought hopefully. *Maybe it's clean and everything is fine and no one will know it ever happened!* She pulled at the ribbon until the dress spilled out in front of her. It **WASN'T** okay.

Maisie Mae felt the hope wash out of her as she looked down at her dress, which was pink . . . and purple . . . and red . . . and BLACK.

She gasped as she held it out in front of her.

It was even **WORSE** than before!

The mud and grime from the football kit had mixed in the washing machine to make black splotches, which sat next to the beetroot and Ribena stains. The beautiful pink colour had mostly washed away, and the dress had **SHRUNK** to about half size! There was no way she would be able to wear it to the wedding.

"I'll just have to run away," Maisie said to herself. "There's no other choice." She crept back up to her room. Auntie Flo was having her hair done in the lounge, so Maisie was alone as she fished under her bed for her extra-specially perfectly-pink Barbie lunch box, and began to stuff it with her favourite toys.

She had only managed to get half of her Koala Sylvanian Family set in there, a pad of coloured paper and a glittery pen before it was full. She looked around for something else to carry her most precious things in. Just then she remembered Bethany-next-door's brand-new glittery-pink rucksack. As it would be the **LAST EVER** time that she saw her best friend, maybe Bethany would lend it to her. She grabbed the bridesmaid dress and tiptoed downstairs.

The whole house was **CHAOS**, with people arriving and delivering presents and flowers and things, that no one even noticed as she opened the door and sneaked outside. She let herself into Bethany's back garden through the side gate. Then she passed silently through the back door, charged upstairs, and burst into Bethany's room.

Bethany-next-door was still in her pyjamas, and looked surprised to see Maisie Mae in her bedroom so early.

"How's the dress?" she said, rubbing the sleep from her eyes.

Maisie Mae threw the dress down on the bed and pointed a shaking finger at it.

Bethany looked at the wreckage. She gasped, and her bottom lip wobbled. "Oh! It's . . . not good, is it?" she said.

Bethany's bridesmaid dress was hung up in her wardrobe so they fetched it down and put it on the bed next to Maisie's. The dresses used to look the same, but now they were nothing alike. "What are you going to do?" Bethany whispered.

"I'm going to run away to Australia," said Maisie Mae. "I thought about it a lot on the way over here. It'll be nice and hot, and I won't need to learn another language." She sighed as she looked at the ruined dress. "I just wish I could have been a bridesmaid, just once."

Bethany-next-door didn't say anything for a few seconds, and Maisie could see that she had her thinking face on. It was the same look she gave when their teacher had just put a really tricky sum on the board. She then seemed to brighten up, and smiled like it was the first day of the summer holidays.

"Ooh!" she said, hopping from foot to foot with excitement. "Ooh! Maisie, you don't need to go to Australia!" Bethany-next-door grabbed her sparkly pink rucksack and stuffed it with the bridesmaid dress. "If we wish hard enough, then everything will be okay! Wishes *always*

work in the most terribly awful situations like this."

She strapped the rucksack to Maisie Mae's back before she could say anything, pushed her out of the bedroom, and practically chased her down the stairs.

"But—"

"Go and get ready!" Bethany-next-door ordered, pushing her out of the front door. "It's almost time for the wedding!"

Maisie Mae stood on her friend's front step for a moment or two, confused. Bethany had gone **CRAZIER** than Jack when he'd eaten fourteen packets of jelly babies for a bet.

"**MAISIE MAE!**" She looked up to see Mum leaning out of an upstairs window. "What on earth are you doing down there? Come here this instant and put your dress on! The guests will be arriving any minute!"

The window slammed shut and Maisie hurried into the house, which was even more manic now. Dad was rushing around with a long to-do list from Mum, and caterers had taken over the kitchen, shouting at each other in big white hats. Maisie peered through and glimpsed the wedding cake, a **GINORMOUS** tower of five white cakes stacked on top of each other with ribbons and rose petals. Maisie Mae's mouth fell open.

"Maisie! Get dressed!" ordered Mum.

Arthur Stanley was clinging to her hip in a tiny version of the pink pageboy suit, looking clean and tidy for once.

Maisie went upstairs and sat down on her bed with a sigh.

Maybe, she thought, *just maybe, Bethany-next-door was right*. She shut her eyes and made the biggest wish she had ever made. Bigger than all her birthday wishes put together.

Reaching into the pink rucksack, she held her breath and pulled out—

—a perfectly pink, completely **CLEAN**, beautiful bridesmaid dress!

Bethany was right! Wishing hard enough had fixed **EVERYTHING!**

CHAPTER TEN

Happily Ever After

Maisie Mae climbed into her spotless dress excitedly. It was perfect!

"Maisie Mae!" shouted Jack. "Mum says if you don't get down here now, you can forget about . . . **WOAH!**"

Jack and the twins gaped at her in awe as she carefully came down the stairs, grinning from ear to ear. She collected her posy of flowers and joined her brothers.

"What . . . Where did you . . .

HOW?" stuttered Josh. Everyone was staring at Maisie Mae as if she was a ghost. Ollie even poked her with his finger to make sure she was real.

"It was magic," said Maisie with a huge smile. "*Wishing* magic!"

Harry and Oliver gasped as the front door opened. They pointed to the figure behind Maisie Mae with a look of horror on their faces.

"I don't think it was wishing that fixed your dress, Maisie!" said Oliver.

"It was *Bethany-next-door*!" said Harry.

Maisie turned to see her best friend come through the door with a smile on her face. She was wearing a shrunken, stained, washed and drained pink bridesmaid dress. Behind her was her mum, who looked very angry indeed.

"Bethany!" Maisie Mae gasped as she realised what was going on. "Oh! You . . . you didn't?"

Bethany-next-door nodded slowly in an *Oh-yes-I-certainly-did* kind of way. She had switched dresses!

Maisie Mae rushed over to see her friend.

"Bethany, why did you swap the dresses?" she whispered. "Now you won't get to be a bridesmaid!"

"No," said Bethany-next-door with a smile. "But *you* will, and that's what's most important."

Maisie gasped and felt her eyes fill with tears.

"Don't cry!" Bethany told her bravely. "I've been a bridesmaid twice before, remember?"

"Come on, boys, into a nice line, like we rehearsed!" Mum said as she burst into the room. "Maisie Mae, you're in front, and Bethany— **OH MY GOODNESS!**" The look of shock on Mum's face was the same as the time that the twins brought a pet tarantula home in their lunchbox. Bethany's mum rushed forward.

"I am *so* sorry! I have no **IDEA** how she got it so messy!" she apologised, red-faced with embarrassment. "She can't be in the wedding looking like this, it'll ruin the day."

"Oh, no, we can sort something out!" said Mum, looking at the dress frantically as if she could clean it with her eyes.

Suddenly Maisie had an idea that was so **BIG** and so **BRILLIANT** that it could solve all the problems.

"The princess dressing-up-dress!" she burst out. "The one your grandparents got you, Bethany. It's big and ruffly and pink!"

"It *is* a similar colour. . ." Bethany's mum agreed.

"It'll have to do," Mum made a snap decision. "Flo's so over-excited. If we're lucky, she won't even notice."

Maisie gave Bethany a huge hug. "Thank you!" Maisie whispered in her friend's ear, before Bethany was whisked away next door to change.

Maisie Mae paced up and down at the bottom of the stairs while she waited for Bethany-next-door to get back.

"If she's not back soon, we'll have to start without her," said Mum.

"She'll be back," said Maisie confidently. There was no way she was going to be a bridesmaid without her best friend there at her side.

Just then there was a creak from the stairs. Auntie Flo was coming! Maisie looked out of the window and saw Bethany and her mum rushing across the garden from next-door. Bethany's pink dressing up dress looked perfect. It was a bit rufflier than Maisie's dress, and there was a picture of the princess at the front, but it was big and floaty and pink.

Bethany raced back over to stand next to Maisie Mae. Mum quickly found some pink ribbon left over from the wedding decorations and tied it over the picture of the princess.

"Close enough," she nodded. "And just in time."

Maisie and Bethany both looked up the stairs as Auntie Flo carefully walked down them, holding up her **HUGE** white dress.

"Eeeekkkkk!" Auntie Flo squealed
when she saw them, and Maisie felt
a sinking feeling. She reached out and
squeezed Bethany-next-door's hand.
Whatever happened, they were in it
together.

"You both look *gorgeous*!" Auntie Flo
continued. "Your dress looks extra ruffly,
Bethany," she said distractedly. "I'm so
lucky to have two

beautiful princesses with me. You look dazzling!"

"So do you!" smiled Maisie Mae. She and Bethany grinned at each other and picked up the hem of Auntie Flo's dress with their spare hands. As the music started, they followed Auntie Flo through the house. Josh, Jack, Harry and Oliver all shuffled behind them.

Maisie peeked over her shoulder and giggled.

Her brothers actually looked like they were *enjoying* themselves! Harry and Ollie were strutting down the aisle, making the guests laugh. Josh and Jack followed behind, each holding one of Arthur Stanley's pudgy hands as he toddled along. They all walked down the garden and up to Maisie's new Uncle Jean-Paul, who wore a smart suit with a brilliant **PINK** tie. As they walked through the guests, everyone turned and smiled, and Maisie and Bethany smiled back. Maisie squeezed her best friend's hand happily.

The wedding was extra-perfect. There was singing and speeches, and Mum even got up to read a bit from a book

that was Auntie Flo's favourite when they were little. Well, she read the first part, and sort of blubbed her way through the last bit, which made Auntie Flo cry too. The bride and groom said their vows to each other, and then said some more words in French, and when they finally kissed, everyone erupted into such loud applause that it drowned out the sound of Ollie and Harry making sick noises.

Once the ceremony was over, Josh, Jack, Harry and Oliver stood on their seats and pelted Auntie Flo and Uncle Jean-Paul with handfuls of colourful confetti.

"Let's **PARTY!**" screamed Auntie

Flo, and music pounded
out of Josh's biggest speakers.
Auntie Flo and Uncle Jean-Paul took the
first dance, but were soon joined by
all the guests on the dance floor. Even
Josh ended up dancing around
with Mum. Harry and
Oliver jumped up and
down like they were
at a rock concert,
and Arthur
Stanley sat on
Jack's shoulders,
delightedly dribbling
into his hair. Dad
bopped in

between everyone, holding a camcorder so he could make a video to embarrass people with later on. Maisie Mae grabbed Bethany-next-door for a dance, and they both kicked off their shoes so they could super-slide across the shiny floor.

After a song where Maisie and Bethany twirled each other around so much that they thought they were going to be sick, Auntie Flo took hold of the microphone.

"Time to throw the bouquet!" she said. "I want all the girls lined up!"

All the girl guests huddled together to see who would catch the bouquet of flowers.

Auntie Flo faced away from them, and they gave a countdown.

"THREE! TWO! ONE! GO!"

Maisie watched as the gorgeous flowers sailed over Auntie Flo's head. It was like it was in slow motion, tumbling round and round. Maisie's eyes went wide as she realised it was heading straight for her! She reached out and caught the flowers by the stems, then held them above her head like a trophy. Everyone cheered, and Maisie felt a happy, warm feeling come over her.

"Well done!" said Bethany-next-door. Maisie Mae didn't say anything, but just gave the flowers to her best-friend-who-was-almost-as-good-as-a-sister.

Bethany grinned a bigger-than-ever grin. "Thank you, Maisie Mae!"

The two friends hugged each other tightly and skipped out of the tent, down the garden path, which was twinkling with fairy lights.

"Well, Maisie Mae? What was your day as a perfect-bridesmaid-princess like?" asked Bethany-next-door.

"It was **AMAZING!**" Maisie Mae said, twirling round until the fairy lights span prettily. "In fact, there's only one thing better than being a perfect-bridesmaid-princess."

"**REALLY?**" Bethany-next-door asked, her eyes wide. "What's that?"

Maisie giggled as she grabbed her friend's hand and they span round together. "Having a brilliant best friend like **YOU!**"

Join Maisie Mae's

NO BOYS ALLOWED CLUB

Sign up at www.lbkids.co.uk/noboysallowed
for free books, competition prizes,
news and more!

READ MORE FROM MAISIE MAE!

ISBN 978-0-349-00153-1

ISBN 978-0-349-00155-5

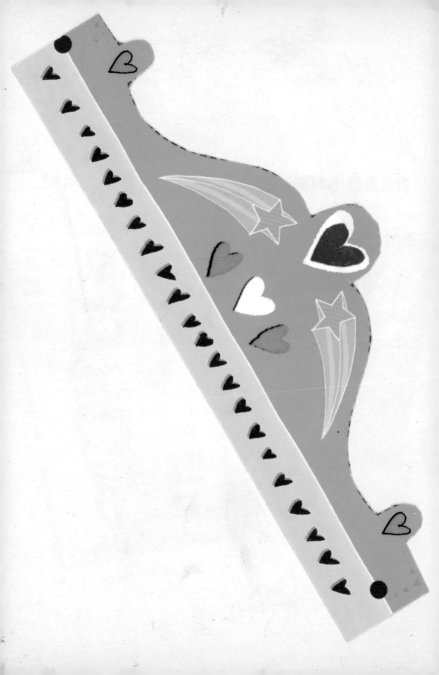